THE
True Gift

Also by Patricia MacLachlan

· · ·

Edward's Eyes

The True Gift

Waiting for the Magic

White Fur Flying

THE True Gift

Patricia MacLachlan

Illustrated by Brian Floca

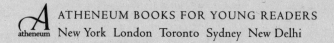

ATHENEUM BOOKS FOR YOUNG READERS
atheneum New York London Toronto Sydney New Delhi

Ⱥ
atheneum

ATHENEUM BOOKS FOR YOUNG READERS

An imprint of Simon & Schuster Children's Publishing Division1230 Avenue of the Americas, New York, New York 10020

This book is a work of fiction. Any references to historical events, real people, or real places are used fictitiously. Other names, characters, places, and events are products of the author's imagination, and any resemblance to actual events or places or persons, living or dead, is entirely coincidental.

Text copyright © 2009 by Patricia MacLachlan

Illustrations copyright © 2009 by Brian Floca

All rights reserved, including the right of reproduction in whole or in part in any form.

Atheneum Books for Young Readers is a registered trademark of Simon & Schuster, Inc.

Atheneum logo is a trademark of Simon & Schuster, Inc.

For information about special discounts for bulk purchases, please contact Simon & Schuster Special Sales at 1-866-506-1949 or business@simonandschuster.com.

The Simon & Schuster Speakers Bureau can bring authors to your live event.

For more information or to book an event, contact the Simon & Schuster Speakers Bureau at 1-866-248-3049 or visit our website at www.simonspeakers.com.

Also available in an Atheneum Books for Young Readers hardcover edition

Book design by Jessica Handelman

The text for this book is set in Venetian 301BT.

The illustrations for this book are rendered in graphite and ebony pencil.

Manufactured in the United States of America

0122 OFF

First Atheneum Books for Young Readers paperback edition October 2013

8   10   9   7

The Library of Congress has cataloged the hardcover edition as follows:

MacLachlan, Patricia.

The true gift : a Christmas story / Patricia MacLachlan ;
illustrated by Brian Floca.—1st ed.

p. cm.

Summary: While spending Christmas at their grandparents' farm, Lily becomes convinced that her younger brother Liam is right about White Cow being lonely and helps him seek a companion for her, leaving little time for Christmas preparations or reading.

ISBN 978-1-4169-9081-9 (hardcover)

[1. Brothers and sisters—Fiction. 2. Cows—Fiction. 3. Books and reading—Fiction. 4. Grandparents—Fiction. 5. Christmas—Fiction.
6. Farm life—Fiction.] I. Floca, Brian, ill. II. Title.

PZ7.M2225Tru 2009

[Fic]—dc22   2009000375

ISBN 978-1-4424-8858-8 (paperback)

ISBN 978-1- 4391-5617-9 (eBook)

This is for John; Pony and Ella; Jamie and Lauren; and Emily, Dean, and Sofia. Love to you all.

With special thanks to Donna Cowan

—P. M.

THE
True Gift

White Cow stood alone in the big meadow.

Her eyes were sad, though she might not have known what sad was. She looked down the road searching for something.

There was a time when she had company, a donkey the color of biscuits, but the farmer who owned the donkey had taken her away.

Sometimes a red fox came to drink from the stream. Sometimes deer came through the meadow to nibble crab apples left on the tree by the barn.

Crows clattered overhead.

But most days White Cow stood alone in the big meadow.

Chapter One

Liam and I sit on the backseat of Papa's old car. The car heater isn't working, so Liam and I share a blanket. We can see our breath in the air.

"How many books did you bring?" whispers Liam.

Liam and I share a worry. Our school closes for ten days, and we're going to Grandpa and Gran's house. We always go there in December, waiting for Christmas and Mama and Papa to come Christmas Day. We worry about not taking as many books as we'll need.

"I brought fifteen books," I say.

"I brought thirty-seven," says Liam.

I burst out laughing.

"Don't worry, Lily. There is the stone library if you run out."

Liam runs out of books all the time. Sometimes he reads three chapter books in one day.

I smile.

We love that stone library, our second home at Grandpa and Gran's farm.

"The lilac library," Liam says.

It's true. No matter what time of year—winter or summer or fall or spring—that library smells like lilacs.

Liam takes a book out of the bag at his feet. I smile. I am three years older than Liam, and I have a sudden sweet memory of teaching him how to read. He was four years old and he grinned for two weeks when he figured out the mystery of words.

"We'll have snow," says Papa, looking up at the sky. Liam and I laugh, and Mama laughs too. We call Papa the Weather Man.

And suddenly, as if his words bring it on, snow begins to fall; flakes one by one, slowly at first, then harder. Papa turns on the windshield wipers, and we watch the back-and-forthing of them.

"I hope the library stays open if it snows," says Liam.

"That library is always open," says Mama. "That library has been open ever since I was a little girl."

We turn into the long dirt driveway to Grandpa and Gran's house, past the meadow where White Cow turns her head to watch us go by.

"Where's Rosie?" asks Liam. "Where's the donkey?"

"Don't know," says Mama. "Can't see her."

The snow is coming harder now and is

beginning to stick to the road. It is almost dusk.

"Did you bring your money?" asks Liam.

I nod.

We have worked weekends and after school to earn money for Christmas presents. I babysat for the three Cooper children across the street. Liam and I both mowed lawns and shoveled snow when it came. Once he painted a shed. There are only two stores in Gran and Grandpa's small town. But that is enough for us to buy presents for everyone.

Liam holds up a red sock with a gray stripe. It is fat with his money.

I smile. The car passes the barn and pulls up to the front porch of the big white house. There are Christmas lights in every window. Gran and Grandpa come out to wave. Their terriers, Emmet and Charlie, bark fiercely at us, then race down the porch steps happily for jumping and licking.

Snow falls harder.

We're here!

Chapter Two

We eat turkey and potatoes and green beans and salad.

"Charlie!" Grandpa's voice is loud.

Emmet scurries under the table.

Charlie stands on hind legs at the counter, trying to lick a pie sitting there. He turns his head to look at Grandpa.

We laugh.

"Once Charlie hopped up on my chair

and ate my dinner," says Grandpa, getting up and making Charlie lie down. "When I went to the door to pay the paperboy."

"He is lured by food," says Gran, smiling. "He doesn't care if we speak sharply to him."

"Emmet does," says Liam.

"That is because Emmet is *thinking* about sneaking our food too," says Grandpa. "Emmet has a conscience."

"Where's Rosie, the donkey?" says Liam. "I didn't see her."

"She went back to her own home," Gran says. "Her owner bought more land, so he has room for her now."

"I miss her," says Grandpa.

"What about White Cow?" asks Liam. "Does she miss Rosie, too?"

Gran, Mama, and Papa get up to clear the dishes from the table.

"Don't know what cows think," says Grandpa.

Charlie follows them, and Emmet comes out from under the dining room table to follow too.

"I can't say that I can read the mind of a cow either," says Gran. "Cows aren't pets, you know. Like Charlie and Emmet. They're different."

"I don't think she's eating as well as she used to, though," says Grandpa at the kitchen sink. He begins to cut the pie.

"We used to have a little herd of cows," he says. "I liked those cows. They were funny and strangely intelligent."

"All eyes and big flat faces," says Gran.

"What happened to the herd?" Liam asks.

"Oh, we sold the cows to people who wanted them for their herds," says Gran.

"Well, what about White Cow?" asks Liam.

"Yes," says Grandpa, smiling at Gran. "What *about* White Cow? Where did she come from?"

"Somewhere," says Gran, waving her hand as if waving away the talk. "She came from somewhere."

The subject was closed. But not for Liam.

"Do we know if she's lonely?" Liam asks.

"Well, she has that whole beautiful meadow all to herself," Gran says. "That's good for a cow."

Liam frowns.

"Maybe that isn't good enough," says Liam softly.

Everyone turns to look at Liam.

A sudden trickle of dread comes over me.

"Let's have pie!" says Gran, trying to be cheerful.

"What do you want for Christmas,

Mom?" asks Mama. Gran drops a coffee mug and it shatters on the floor.

"A coffee mug," she says, making Mama laugh.

A Christmas tree stands between the dining room and living room, waiting for us to decorate it. It has only little white lights on it now. The white lights could be stars in a winter sky. I steal a look at Liam, and he is staring at his pie. I know him. He will think and think and think about White Cow alone in the meadow. Those thoughts of his will flow out like smoke, surrounding us all. He will spoil our vacation. I know this.

I kick him under the table, and he looks up, startled.

He smiles. "Pie!" he says too cheerfully.

I know Liam. Liam is not thinking about pie.

Dinner is over. Mama and Papa are getting ready to drive home.

"We'll be back Christmas Day," says Mama. "Don't let them get away with any more than I do," she says to Gran. "I wish we could stay."

Gran smiles. She likes this time with us as much as we like being alone with her and Grandpa in the house.

"Where's Liam?" asks Mama.

We look around.

Suddenly, I know where Liam is. I know

where Liam always is when we visit Grandpa and Gran.

"I'll find him," I say.

I take my coat from a hook by the door and go outside to the porch. It has snowed more since we first got here, and I can see Liam's footprints in the snow down the sidewalk. I follow them to the driveway, then across to the paddock gate. There is a slice of moon above. And then I see Liam, standing just inside the fence next to White Cow. Some of the moonlight falls on White Cow, making her look like a marble statue. She looks at me as I walk up to the fence.

Liam turns and looks at me too. "She's lonely," he says.

"She's a cow," I say. "Cows don't care."

Liam turns back to White Cow. He strokes her side, then he turns and opens the gate. He walks past me up to the house.

White Cow stares at me.

"You're a cow," I whisper to her. "Just a cow."

Chapter Three

Mama and Papa have gone. It is quiet in the house.

My bedroom overlooks the short dirt road that winds down to the town with its two markets and the elementary school, the post office and the lilac library. Liam's bedroom overlooks the meadow, the big barn, and White Cow.

The moon is higher when I walk into

Liam's room. Liam is looking out at the meadow. Snow has dusted everything, and the moon outlines trees and bushes and the shining brook that runs through the fields.

"Liam?" I say softly.

He turns. "What?"

"You know what, Liam? We're going to take walks and read books and shop for Christmas gifts for everyone and help Grandpa and Gran and go to the library. We're going to have fun! Right?"

Liam looks at me steadily, the same look he had when he was four years old, trying to figure out how to read.

"Right," he says. He turns back to look out over the meadow.

"And feed White Cow," he adds. "I always feed White Cow. And Rosie, when she was here."

"Liam?"

I speak more softly because I've hurt his feelings.

"What?"

"You are a worrier."

Liam turns to look at me. "So are you."

"White Cow is fine. She is happy in the field and the barn," I say.

"Maybe," says Liam.

Then he turns to take his books out of his book bags and stack them, one by one by one, on bookshelves by his bed.

"Maybe," he repeats.

*　　*　　*

In the morning there is sun. It pours in my window, tumbling across the quilt. I can smell coffee and breakfast downstairs.

Gran and Grandpa are at the kitchen table.

"Morning, Lily," says Gran. "There is juice and fresh muffins."

"Good morning. Where's Liam?"

"He's in my study," says Grandpa. "I have to go to work now. There must be some news somewhere to print." Grandpa works at the newspaper in town.

He kisses the top of my head. "Want to come to work with me, Lambie?"

Grandpa is the only person in the world who calls me Lambie.

"I am going to walk to town later," I say. "Liam will come too."

"He's pretty busy in there, Lily," says Gran. "You may never dig him out."

Liam is surrounded by Grandpa's books and papers. He stares at a large book open in front of him.

"What are you doing?" My voice seems loud in the quiet room.

Liam jumps and closes the book with a thump. "Nothing."

I know that tone. I know Liam.

"Show me," I say. "You might as well show me."

"You won't like it."

"I know I won't. Show me."

I pull up a chair and sit close to him.

Liam sighs and opens the book. He thumbs through the pages and then stops.

And there it is. I lean over and read.

Cows are social beings. Cows have feelings. They have been known to bear grudges. They live in families and are capable of grief, loss, and loneliness.

I look at Liam.

"There's more," he says.

I shake my head. I reach over and close the book.

"I have to do something about White Cow," says Liam.

I am suddenly so angry that I can hardly think of what words to say.

"You dumb boy!" I say. "You are so . . . dumb! I was right. You will spoil Christmas. It will be all your fault."

Liam gives me that steady look. "I have to do something," he says again. "You can blame me. You can blame White Cow if you want."

Liam opens the book again, ignoring me.

I feel surprising tears in my eyes.

Liam pays no attention to me.

Liam reads some more. Then he looks at me.

"I think we should walk to town," he says.

"Why?" I say.

"Because that is what we do when we come here at Christmas," he says.

I can't think of anything to say.

Chapter Four

We put on our coats and hats and mittens in the warm kitchen.

"We're going to see White Cow first," Liam tells Gran.

"I thought you probably would," she says. She hands me some money. "This is for butter at the market. And these letters are to be mailed."

Outside it is cold and bright. It feels like

frost on my nose. We walk down the length of the fence, looking for White Cow.

"She's not in the meadow," says Liam. His breath comes out in puffs in the winter air.

We open the gate and walk through the snow-covered grass to the barn.

The barn is old and smells like hay and the winter breath of all the animals that have lived there. We stop as we enter, both of us, because it is huge. The roof is so high, it reminds me of the picture of a cathedral I once saw in a book. There are stalls and many bales of hay and barrels with covers that hold grain. Parts of the floor are old wood, and our boots slip on

the smoothness. Slices of light from the windows fall across the wood.

"White Cow!" calls Liam suddenly.

There is a shuffle of noise at the far end of the barn, and White Cow walks out of a stall. She slowly walks toward us. She stops. She is so big and white.

Liam talks to her in his soft voice. "Poor girl. Good girl. Come, girl."

White Cow comes close and suddenly leans against Liam. He is almost knocked off his feet by this affection. But he doesn't fall.

My heart beats faster.

"Lily?" His voice comes from some-where behind White Cow.

"You're scared," he says. "She's just big. She can't help it."

Scared? Am I? Am I scared?

"Come closer, Lily."

I walk closer and reach out a hand and stroke her long white side. *She is warm.* She turns to look at me for a moment, and I am surprised by her eyes.

We stay with White Cow a long time in the sweet-smelling barn. And when we finally walk to the barn door so we can go to town, White Cow follows us, standing in the doorway. More than once we turn, walking backward, and see White Cow watching us from the barn, the doorway framing her like a picture frame.

We are mostly silent as we walk down the road, down the hill, past several houses that are scattered along the way, past a field bordered by red barberry bushes.

"I was right," I say softly. "Nothing is the same now."

Liam doesn't answer me.

"Nothing."

Liam still doesn't speak.

"How did you know I was scared of White Cow?" I ask finally.

I turn to look at him.

"I just knew. You don't know her the way I do," he says.

We walk quietly. The fields are snow coated; the only green, the spruces and white pines in the fields. The sky is gray.

"We have to buy a cow," says Liam as we come to the center of town.

I stop walking, but Liam walks on.

"You can't do that! You're just a kid."

A girl on a horse comes up the hill, the horse peering closely at me, its hooves quiet on the snow-covered road.

I run to catch up with Liam. We walk together, not speaking.

I take a breath and know that I'll be sorry that I ask the question I'm going to ask.

"How can we buy a cow?"

Liam turns and grins brightly at me. "I don't know," he says. "But we will."

Chapter Five

Lisa, the librarian, is happy to see us at the lilac library.

"Two whole weeks of nonstop reading, right?" she says. "I wish everyone read the way you two do."

Liam disappears in the stacks, and I look at the shelves of books; books and books and books. Liam comes back with a nonfiction book with the title *The Emotional Life of Cows* and checks it out.

We mail Gran's letters at the post office.

"Wait," says Liam, stopping. He studies the notices on the bulletin board:

LOST CAT: Name is Thug.

Not lovable. Reward.

. . .

WANTED: Exotic chickens

for breeding.

. . .

WANTED: A quiet room by the

river for one person and the most

intelligent dog in the world.

Liam looks at the notices for so long, I finally tug at his coat.

"Wait," says Liam again. "I'm having a thought. Go ahead. I'll catch up with you."

I go outside and walk to the market. Liam comes up from behind me with a look.

"What?" I ask.

"Just thinking."

The market has newly polished wood floors, and we wander down the aisles until we find butter for Gran.

Next door there is a new small store called Already Read Books. A sign on the door says SECONDHAND BOOKS BOUGHT

AND SOLD. Liam puts his face close to the window and peers in because it is closed.

"Books," he says happily.

We go to the general store. It is filled with dishes and jewelry and toys and penny candy and kitchen gadgets and cakes and pies and muffins. Blown-glass Christmas balls hang from the ceiling; angels and stars for the top of the tree sit on shelves.

"Look," I tell Liam. "A new coffee cup for Gran."

I hold up a white mug with a great blue heron painted on.

Liam shakes his head. "Wait," says Liam. "Don't buy it yet."

"Wait for what?"

Liam doesn't answer.

I put the mug back and stare at Liam.

"We're going to have Christmas whether you want it or not, you know."

I walk out of the store and past the post office and past the small coffee shop. Past the Already Read store. I turn up the road to Gran's. I am close to tears for the second time today. I wish Liam would not think so much. I wish White Cow could go away and not come back so I wouldn't have to think about her.

There is the sound of pounding feet behind me.

"Hey," says Liam, panting from running.

"I don't like you," I say, bursting into tears at last.

"I know. I don't like me either," says Liam.

I stare at Liam and I can't help it. I start laughing and crying at the same time.

"I'm just a kid, Lily," says Liam. "You said so yourself."

We walk on.

"Cows cost a lot," says Liam. "Five hundred dollars sometimes."

"We can't afford that," I say.

"Maybe a young cow," Liam says.

"Called a calf," I say, starting to laugh again.

Liam laughs too. And for a while it is

the way it used to be. The way all other Christmases at Gran and Grandpa's house have been.

Liam scoops up snow and tries to stuff it down my neck. Ice on the trees sparkles in the sunlight. We pick some red barberry branches for Gran.

But when we get home, White Cow is still there, standing by the fence, watching us with those eyes.

It is not the way it used to be.

Chapter Six

All through dinner there is no talk of White Cow. There is talk of Christmas and the town and books.

"Do you want to make Christmas cookies tomorrow, Lily?" asks Gran.

"Sure," I say.

Charlie sits by Grandpa's feet, watching the floor intently, waiting for Grandpa to drop food. Emmet sleeps by the fireplace, almost *in* the fireplace.

Liam gets up and carries his plate to the kitchen and comes back for the other plates.

"Do you have a copy machine?" he asks Grandpa.

"Nope. Sorry," says Grandpa.

"I'll keep thinking," he says in a soft voice.

"Don't think," I tell him just as softly.

Liam smiles.

That night we sleep with the curtains open so we can look out and see the stars across the sky. I wake in the night once and can see light under the door of

Liam's room. I sigh and turn over and count the stars until I fall back to sleep.

"Where is Liam?" I ask at breakfast the next morning.

Grandpa laughs. "You're always asking that, Lambie. He went off early. He seems to have plans."

I pour a glass of juice. "Yes. Liam always has plans," I say.

Gran and I make cookies all morning: Christmas trees with silver ball decorations; snowmen with red cinnamon buttons; star cookies and moon cookies; and little house cookies with frosted doors and windows.

"This is nice, Gran. Like it always is."

"It is, Lily. Maybe you and Liam can come this summer and help cut the hayfield and plant gardens."

I smile at Gran. That would be good. But there is something about Christmas here.

"There is," says Gran. And I realize that I have said my thoughts out loud.

Gran puts the cookies on a big platter. "Beautiful," she says.

"I'm going to look for Liam," I tell Gran.

"There are more letters to mail on the table, Lily."

I put on my boots and coat and walk out to the driveway.

White Cow is standing by the gate, an empty black bucket at her feet. I walk over to her.

"Did Liam give you grain?" I ask. "Sure he did," I whisper. I smile at myself, talking to a cow.

After a moment I reach out and touch White Cow's neck. She stares at me as if she knows me.

"I'll be back," I tell her.

And then what I say to White Cow surprises me.

"Don't worry," I whisper. "We'll take care of you."

And I walk off down the driveway and down the road, past houses and fields and the stream I hear flowing. When I come into the center of town, I go to the post office to mail Gran's letters.

And there, on the bulletin board, I see the first notice. I know what Liam has been doing.

WANTED: A cow friend for a lonely, sad cow. It is Christmas and she needs a friend. Think how you'd feel. I'm buying. Call Liam.

He has written Gran and Grandpa's telephone number at the bottom.

I look at the notice for a long time, then drop Gran's letters in the mail slot.

I walk across the street looking for Liam.

There, nailed to the telephone pole by the lilac library, is another notice.

ONCE UPON A TIME
THERE WAS A WHITE COW,
ALL ALONE, AT CHRISTMAS.
SHE WAS SAD AND LONELY.
SHE LIVES ON SOUTH STREET.
IF YOU HAVE A COW FRIEND
FOR HER, PLEASE CALL LIAM.

I smile a little and walk across the street.

In the market window is another notice.

I feel like I am following Liam by his notices,
like following his footprints in the snow.

HELP WHITE COW.

SELL ME A FRIEND FOR

HER FOR CHRISTMAS.

CALL LIAM.

YOUR CHRISTMAS WILL

BE HAPPIER, TOO.

I find Liam, tacking up a notice on the
notice board at the general store. This one
has a drawing of a white cow with a tear in
her eye.

"You've been busy," I say.

Liam nods.

I take a deep breath. "I can't believe that I'm going to say this, Liam. I'm proud of you."

Liam smiles.

"Let's go home," he says wearily.

He takes my hand and we walk around the corner and start up the hill that begins South Street. Little flakes of snow begin to fall. Before long there is steady snow. I look up and watch the snow come down.

"Liam?"

"What?"

"I talked to White Cow this morning."

Liam doesn't speak for a moment. And when he does, what he says makes me smile.

"You're turning into me," he says.

We walk all the way home and the snow grows heavier. And when we walk up the driveway to Gran and Grandpa's house, past the barn, past White Cow, Gran comes to the door and tells us there has been a telephone call for Liam.

Chapter Seven

Snow is still falling when we leave. Gran looks at us, knowing that we're not telling her things.

"Something's going on, right?" she says.

"Right," Liam and I answer at the same time.

"Well, I'm not asking you about it right now," she says. "Right now," she repeats.

Liam grins at her and pulls me out the front door.

The sky has darkened and the world is full of snow.

"Who is it?" I ask.

"Thomas says his father is selling their calf. He said he'd tell me about it when I get there."

The snow is so heavy that we almost miss the West Street turn. We walk fast, and then ahead, in the dense falling snow, is a boy.

"Thomas?" calls Liam.

Thomas turns. "Yes."

Several cows are in the meadow. One small brown calf stands by the fence.

"I'm Liam. This is Lily."

Thomas takes a folded paper out of his pocket. It is one of Liam's notices.

"Did you write this?" asks Thomas.

"I did. We're looking for a cow."

Thomas looks at the brown calf.

"Is that yours?" asks Liam.

"Yes, but you're too late. My father says she's sold."

"Sold? To live where?" asks Liam.

"For the market," says Thomas softly. "For meat."

"For meat!" says Liam.

There is a moment of silence, no sounds at all, like when the wind suddenly stops blowing.

"For meat?" repeats Liam, trying to understand.

Thomas nods. "Papa says we need the money."

"Liam, the calf is sold," I say. I shiver in the cold. "I'm going home. I'm freezing."

"Wait a minute, Lily," says Liam. "Thomas, how much is your Papa selling the calf for?"

Thomas shrugs. "A couple hundred dollars, I think. For Christmas money," he adds.

"Two hundred," says Liam. He takes Thomas's arm.

"Listen, Thomas. I'm going to save your calf. What's her name?"

Thomas shrugs again. "She doesn't have a name. We call her—"

"Brown Cow," finishes Liam happily.

Thomas looks surprised. "Yes. How did you know that?"

I know what Liam is thinking. I start walking away. I walk on until suddenly Liam is beside me.

"Don't talk," I say, loving and hating him at the same time.

Well, "hate" is a strong word. So is "love."

One good thing, though: He doesn't speak all the way home through the falling snow.

Chapter Eight

Liam and I sit in his room, going through our money.

Charlie and Emmet sit on the bed, watching the counting closely, as if the money will turn into food. When it stays money, Charlie gets bored and turns over on his back, with his feet in the air. Emmet leans over to chew Charlie's chin.

Liam empties his sock. He has $67.50.
I have $76.00.

"That comes to . . . ," I begin.

"One forty-three fifty," says Liam, who
is quick with numbers. "That isn't enough."

"Maybe we could ask Mama and Papa,
or Gran and Grandpa."

Liam shakes his head. "No. I want to do
this."

"You are stubborn."

"Yes."

Liam goes to the window. "Maybe we
could get jobs," he says.

"What kind of jobs?" I ask. "We only
have a few days left. And we don't know
when the calf will be sold."

"Brown Cow," corrects Liam.

"Brown Cow," I repeat. I would smile, but I do not feel happy.

Liam paces the room, thinking Liam thoughts.

"Maybe . . . ," I begin.

"Wait!" says Liam loudly.

I jump. Charlie and Emmet sit up.

Liam grabs one of his book bags and begins packing his books.

"Get that bag, Lily. Start packing."

"But, Liam——"

"Pack!" says Liam loudly.

I've never heard him speak loudly before.

I pack.

"What are we doing?" I ask.

"The Already Read secondhand book-store in town," says Liam, as if I should know what he's about to do.

"What about it?"

Liam packs the last book.

"I'm going to sell my books," he says.

My mouth opens.

Liam holds up his hand.

"Let's go. Can you carry that bag?"

I lift a bag with a dozen books in it.

"I can."

Liam leaves the room with his bags of books. He doesn't look back at me. Charlie and Emmet jump down from the bed and follow. They don't look back at me either.

✷   ✷   ✷

"Where are you going?" calls Gran.

Liam and I walk out on the porch lugging our load of books.

"We have an errand in town," calls Liam. "We'll be home before dinner."

"I'm going to drive you," calls Gran. "There's too much snow." She puts on her jacket and comes out with Charlie and Emmet. We all climb in the car.

"Don't worry," Gran says to Liam, "I won't ask what you're doing."

Liam and I smile.

We see White Cow outside the barn, turning her big white head to watch us drive by.

"Liam, these are your books. You love these books," I whisper to him.

"If I can get a couple of dollars a book, we'll get Brown Cow and still have some money left over for Christmas," he whispers back.

"I don't even care about Christmas presents anymore," I say out loud, surprising myself.

"Me neither," says Liam, grinning.

"Me neither," says Gran in the front seat, making us laugh because we have forgotten she was there.

We park in front of the Already Read bookstore.

"Stay here," says Liam.

He takes the bags and leaves us in the car. There is silence. Charlie and Emmet climb into the front seat with Gran.

"All right," says Gran. "You are my captive, Lily."

"You promised you wouldn't ask," I remind her.

"I don't always tell the truth," says Gran, making me laugh.

So I tell her.

Gran is very quiet.

"All for a cow," she says softly.

"For all of us," I say.

"Yes," says Gran. "That's true."

"Don't tell Liam I told you," I say.

"I promise," says Gran.

We both laugh because Gran has already said she doesn't always tell the truth.

We wait. A yellow Lab walks by, and Charlie and Emmet howl.

We wait longer.

And then Liam comes out. He is carrying two empty bags and one with some books in it. He gets into the car.

"Okay," he says, smiling.

"Do we go to Thomas's house?" asks Gran.

Liam looks at Gran and then at me. "You told her," he says.

"She made me," I say.

"Yes," says Liam. "Let's go get Brown Cow."

Chapter Nine

Gran drives to West Street faster than she usually drives. Liam laughs in the backseat, the first time he's laughed like that in a long time.

Gran turns at West Street and stops at Thomas's house. A covered truck is parked there with nothing written on the side.

Thomas is outside, and his father, and a man who holds a rope with Brown Cow at the other end. Liam gets out of the car before Gran stops.

Thomas has been crying. His younger brothers are huddled behind him.

"You're too late, Liam," Thomas says. "Too late. Papa sold her."

"I'm sorry, Liam," says Thomas's father. "But she is sold now."

"But I'll pay you more money!" says Liam.

"Too late," says the man with the rope. He pulls on the rope, but Brown Cow digs her feet in. "Come on," he says crossly. "Come on!" He slaps Brown Cow on the backside, but Brown Cow backs up farther and makes a sad moo. The man reaches inside his truck and takes out a long prod.

"Stop!" cries Thomas.

The prod has a hook at one end, and the man walks up to Brown Cow.

"You'll hurt her," says Thomas loudly. One of his brothers begins to cry.

"Wait," says Thomas's father softly.

Everyone stops and looks at him. Gran gets out of the car and stands next to Liam.

"I don't think I like you," Thomas's father says to the man.

"A deal is a deal!" the man shouts.

"Well, hello there, Jake," says Gran. She speaks as softly as Thomas's father.

"You!" says the man harshly. "You again."

"Yes," says Gran. "Me."

"This woman," he sputters, "she bought a white cow out from under me a long time ago!"

"And I paid much too much money," says Gran.

I look at Gran.

"My secret until now," she says.

"A true gift," Thomas's father says. "Its own reward. I'm sure that cow never thanked you."

Thomas's father holds out the check. "You take this and leave," he says to the man. "Now, please."

The man stares at him, then at Gran.

He grabs the check, muttering, and gets in his truck. He starts his truck and drives off fast.

It is quiet.

Thomas puts his arm around Brown Cow.

Liam holds out the money. "This is for you," he says.

Thomas's father takes it. He doesn't count it. "Thank you," he says. "That was a good thing you did. I don't remember Thomas ever loving a calf this much."

He looks at Thomas with his arm around Brown Cow.

"Thomas can visit this little animal whenever he wants?"

Gran smiles. "Anytime. Every day if he wants," she says.

"Thank you," he says to Gran.

Gran shakes her head. "It was them," she says, meaning Liam and me.

"Mostly Liam," I say. "He sold his books."

Thomas's father swallows as if he might cry. He holds out his hand and shakes Liam's hand. "Merry Christmas," he says.

Liam and Thomas and I walk Brown Cow up the road. It is late afternoon and the light slants across the fields.

"Brown Cow is happy," says Thomas.

~ 70 ~

Liam smiles.

"White Cow will be happy soon," he says.

Cars pass us on their way home or to market. The girl on horseback comes down the road.

"Hello, cow," she says as she goes by.

"Hello, girl on horse," says Liam, making us all laugh.

We pass the field with bright red barberry bushes. We pass a house or two, lights turned on inside. No one has curtains at their windows here, because it is the country. There is no one to look in, only deer and coyotes and once in a while a confused bear that comes out of winter hibernation.

We pass the little brook that flows under the road.

And then we can see the barn at Gran and Grandpa's house.

Grandpa and Gran stand on the porch. They have been waiting for us.

We turn up the long driveway and walk along the fence. Before we reach the gate, White Cow comes out of the barn. She sees us. She moos loudly, and Brown Cow moos back. White Cow runs down to the gate. I've never seen White Cow run before. She moos again and again, and Brown Cow answers her.

Thomas takes the rope from around Brown Cow's neck, and we open the gate.

Brown Cow rushes in, and White Cow begins to lick her all over. She licks Brown Cow for a long time.

And then White Cow lays her head on Brown Cow's head.

"A true gift, like Thomas's father said," says Liam in the softest voice I've ever heard.

Christmas Eve

We have hung decorations on the tree, including two small cows that Grandpa brings; one white, one brown.

Mama and Papa will come tomorrow morning.

White Cow and Brown Cow are close together in the old barn, and Liam and I go to bed; Liam with Emmet, me with Charlie, watching the stars and a huge full moon appearing over the meadow.

"Lily. Lily!"

It's very late when Liam shakes me awake.

"Lily. Something's happening."

"What?" I sit up, frightened. "What's wrong?"

There is the sound of dogs barking somewhere.

There are lights outside and muffled noises, the sound of a truck on the road.

I hear Gran and Grandpa talking downstairs.

"Come," says Liam, pulling me out of bed.

We run downstairs.

The porch light is on.

Grandpa is putting on his coat.

"What's wrong?" I ask.

"Don't know," he says. "I am going out to check. You should stay here."

"I will not," says Gran, putting on her coat and hat.

"I'm coming too," says Liam.

I grab my coat and boots and follow them out the door.

The moon is so bright that the meadow looks white. We walk down the sidewalk and across the driveway to the meadow fence. Our feet crunch in the snow.

"Look!" says Grandpa.

There in the meadow is a small decorated Christmas tree; silver balls and chains gleam in the moonlight.

"Wherever did that come from?" says Gran.

And there is more.

White Cow and Brown Cow turn their heads to look at us. But with them are more cows.

"There," says Grandpa. "And there!"

"And more cows over there!" Liam says.

I can't count all the cows. When they look at us, we can see the moon in their big eyes.

We walk closer.

So many cows. It feels like a dream.

We can't speak.

"What happened?" I ask Grandpa, leaning against him.

Gran picks up a stack of papers. They are Liam's notices.

"The people in town read about White Cow," she says.

"There's a note," says Grandpa.

Merry Christmas,
White Cow. You shouldn't be
alone for Christmas.

"Will all these cows stay here forever?" asks Liam.

"No," says Gran, laughing. "I think this is a Christmas visit."

"A Christmas visitation of cows," says Grandpa with a smile.

"She will always have Brown Cow," says Gran.

We are quiet again, looking at the cows in the snow-covered meadow. All those big faces.

"That is quite a sight," says Grandpa.

"It is," says Gran. She looks at her watch. "It's Christmas," she says.

"I'll say it is," says Grandpa.

"Merry Christmas, White Cow," I call to her.

"Merry Christmas, Brown Cow," calls Liam.

"Merry Christmas, all cows!" says Gran.

And when we walk back to the house and turn to look at the meadow, an ocean of eyes looks back at us in the moonlight.

Take a sneak peek at
Patricia MacLachlan's

fly aWay

Everyone in Lucy's family sings.

Everyone, except Lucy.

Just like singing, helping Aunt Frankie

prepare for flooding season is a

family tradition—even if Frankie

doesn't want help. But when the flood

arrives, Lucy will need to find her

voice to save her little brother.

Secrets

We drive across the Minnesota prairie in our old tan and green Volkswagen bus. My father does not believe in new cars. He loves the old Volkswagen with the top that pops up like a tent. He can take the motor apart and fix it himself.

In the way back are neat wooden

framed beds for sleeping. In a pen are Mama's chickens: Ella, Sofia, and Nickel. Mama loves them and never goes away for long without them. My younger sister, Grace, sits in her car seat next to me. In back of her is Teddy, the youngest, with his stuffed beaver.

My father, called Boots because he wears them, is driving, listening to opera on the radio. It is *La Traviata*.

Misterioso, misterioso altero . . .

I know it well. If a conductor dropped dead on stage I could climb up there and conduct. Now here is something abnormal. I can't sing. When I open my mouth nothing happens. I know the music, but I can't sing it. I can only conduct it.

My father went to Harvard. His parents expected him to be a banker like his father. In secret he planned to be a poet.

But then he discovered cows. He became a farmer.

He loves cows.

"They are poetry, Lucy," he tells me. "I can't write anything better than a cow."

Maggie, my mother in the front seat, wears headphones. I know she is listening to Langhorne Slim. She loves Langhorne Slim as much as my father loves opera. And I know *her* secret. She would like to sing like Langhorne Slim. She would like to *be* Langhorne Slim.

*If you've got worries, then you're
like me. Don't worry now, I
won't hurt you.*

My younger sister, Gracie, ignores the opera and my mother's bopping around in the front seat. Gracie sings in a high perfect voice, fluttering her hands like birds.

*"The birdies fly away, and they come
back home.
The birdies fly away, and they come
back home."*

I turn and look at my little brother, Teddy. He smiles at me and I know what that smile is all about.

In his small head he is singing the "Fly Away" chorus in private so no one can hear.

Fly away, fly away,
All the birdies fly away.

I smile back at him.

This is our secret because Teddy wants it that way.

I have known for a long time that Teddy can sing perfectly in tune even though he is not yet two. We all know he doesn't speak words yet. But only Teddy and I know that he sings. He doesn't sing the words, but sings every song with *"la la la."* He sings to me every night, climbing out of his bed, padding into my room in the dark. He sings a peppy "Baa, Baa,

Black Sheep," ending with a "Yay" at the end with his hands in the air.

"La La La La
LaLaLaLaLa.
Yay!"

He sings a soft, quiet "All The Pretty Horses." *"La, la, la."*

I made a mistake once and told them all—Boots, Mama, and Gracie—that Teddy can sing. They didn't believe me. And of course Teddy wouldn't sing for them. Only for me.

"I've never heard Teddy sing," says Gracie.

"He can't even talk yet," says Mama. "How could he sing?"

Teddy has music but no words.

I have words but no music.

We are a strange pair.

And here is *my* secret: I am planning to be a poet. I have written thirty-one and a half poems. Some are bad. They are bad hideaway poems. I plan to get better and publish better poems and buy Mama more chickens and take Boots to see *La Traviata* at the opera house in New York City, wherever New York City is.

When I get to be a poet Boots will be pleased.

He will be proud.

And one day, for him, I will write a poem as beautiful as a cow.

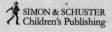

From the Newbery Award–winning author
Patricia MacLachlan

*Find out how four dogs and one cat help one boy
and his sister save their family.*

Also from Patricia MacLachlan

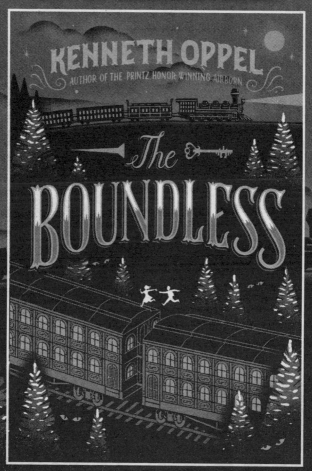

Leon Leyson was only ten years old when the
Nazis invaded Poland and his life changed forever.

THE BOY ON THE WOODEN BOX

How the impossible
became possible...
on Schindler's list

A MEMOIR
LEON LEYSON
with MARILYN J. HARRAN & ELISABETH B. LEYSON

*A legacy of hope from one of the youngest children
on Schindler's list to survive*

athenium